Daniel Learns to Share

adapted by Becky Friedman

based on the screenplay "Daniel Shares His Tigertastic Car"

written by Wendy Harris

poses and layouts by Jason Fruchter

Ready-to-Read

Simon Spotlight

New York London Toronto Sydney New Delhi

I show them my new car.

My car goes *vroom-vroom!*

Prince Wednesday is sad.

My dad tells us
how to share.

I give Prince Wednesday my car.

Now Prince Wednesday
is happy.

My friends play with their cars.

"Here is your car back," says Prince Wednesday.

"We can race our cars!" says Miss Elaina.

Miss Elaina uses a pretend car.

Prince Wednesday gives the truck back.

Miss Elaina is happy.

Daniel Goes Out for Dinner

adapted by Maggie Testa

based on the screenplay "A Night Out at the Restaurant"

written by Becky Friedman

poses and layouts by Jason Fruchter

Ready-to-Read

Simon Spotlight

New York   London   Toronto   Sydney   New Delhi

Hi, neighbor!

We are going out for dinner.

What food do you think looks yummy?

I want the

chicken and broccoli.

Yum!

We tell our waiter
what we want to eat.

Our waiter will bring the food to the table.

Now we have to wait for our food to be cooked.

It is very, very

hard to wait.

"You can play a quiet, sit-down game," says my dad.

"We can play 'what is missing,'" says Katerina.

Look at the things
on the table.

Katerina hides

one of the things.

What is missing?

The salt was missing!

What should we do while we wait?

When you wait,
you can play, sing,
or imagine anything.

We can imagine that the things on the table can play with us!

We do not have to wait anymore.

I am glad I waited
for my food.

It is so yummy!

I can play, sing,

or imagine anything

to make waiting easier.

Friends
Help Each Other

adapted by Farrah McDoogle

based on the screenplay "Friends Help Each Other" written by Wendy Harris

poses and layouts by Jason Fruchter

Ready-to-Read

Simon Spotlight

New York   London   Toronto   Sydney   New Delhi

Hi, neighbor!
Today I am playing
with Katerina Kittycat.

"Meow, Meow!
Do you want to have a
tea party?"
asks Katerina.

"No, thank you," says Katerina. "I can do it all by myself."

Oh no!
Katerina bumps the table
with the chair.

"I made a mess," cries Katerina. "Our tea party is ruined!"

"Maybe Daniel can help!" says Henrietta.

"Teatime!"
says Katerina.

"I want to pour the tea by myself!"

Oh no!
Katerina spills the tea.

I can help clean up
the tea!

Friends help each other, yes they do!

"Yes! But this time I will not do it all by myself!" says Katerina.

"Will you help me pour?" asks Katerina.

I am happy I helped
my friend today!
Ugga Mugga!

Daniel Visits the Library

adapted by Maggie Testa
based on the screenplay "Calm for Storytime"
written by Wendy Harris
poses and layouts by Jason Fruchter

Ready-to-Read

Simon Spotlight
New York   London   Toronto   Sydney   New Delhi

At last it is storytime!

X the Owl reads a book to us.

Prince Wednesday hops like a frog.

I cannot hear the story.

We listen to the story.

X the Owl finishes
the story.

"The end," he says.

Storytime is over. Now we can go outside and play.